For my beloved grandmother, Irene, who always encouraged my dreams. And for my children, Zach and Isabelle, who continuously ignite my imagination.

– Natalia

Copyright © 2023 Clavis Publishing Inc., New York

Visit us on the Web at www.clavis-publishing.com.

A Picture Day to Remember written by Natalia Paruzel-Gibson and illustrated by Nynke Boelens
Contributing editor: Berna Ozunal

ISBN 978-1-60537-728-5

This book was printed in October 2022 at Nikara, M. R. Štefánika 858/25, 963 01 Krupina, Slovakia.

First Edition
10 9 8 7 6 5 4 3 2 1

Written by Natalia Paruzel-Gibson
Illustrated by Nynke Boelens

A PICTURE DAY
TO REMEMBER

Clavis

NEW YORK

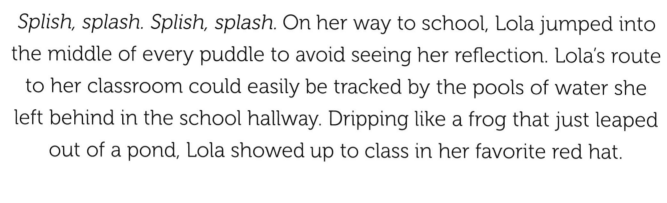

Splish, splash. Splish, splash. On her way to school, Lola jumped into the middle of every puddle to avoid seeing her reflection. Lola's route to her classroom could easily be tracked by the pools of water she left behind in the school hallway. Dripping like a frog that just leaped out of a pond, Lola showed up to class in her favorite red hat.

Larger than an umbrella, the hat cast an enormous shadow over Lola's face. To get to her desk, she needed a classmate to hold the door while she squeezed her hat through. The hat had earned her the nickname *Red*.

Her teacher, Ms. Sung, often asked Lola, "My dear, can you see where you're going with that hat on? Why are you hiding under there? It would be so nice to see more of your adorable face. Please be careful not to bump into anything, Lola."

Sometimes she did bump into things, but wearing the hat every day helped Lola cover her face and avoid any embarrassment. Her hat was like an extra-large, cozy blanket she could easily hide under.

One day, Ms. Sung announced, "Class, just a reminder that today is picture day."

Lola clenched her shoulders and pulled her hat down to hide. "Why, oh why did I forget picture day?" Lola mumbled to herself. Her little heart felt like it was wildly tumbling down a steep hill.

Ever since kindergarten, Lola had avoided coming to school on picture day. She always heard kids say things like, "My mom got me a new sequined dress for picture day" and "My mom promised to braid my hair in the morning" and "I can't wait to wear my pirate tie!" She knew it was a day when everyone was supposed to look their best.

Lola's hands were sweaty. Her skin was tingling with goosebumps, and her face was turning the color of her hat—or at least it felt that way.

Mr. Smirk, the photographer, called on Lola's class to come to the gym. "Okay, kids, time to line up. Why don't we try two rows?" Accidentally, Lola ended up in the front row.

"No one will see me in this picture," said Kate. "I'm completely blocked by Red—or should I say, her giant red hat."

Lola wanted to throw on a magical cloak and just disappear.

"You in the red hat—I'm sorry, I don't know your name—can you please take your hat off for the picture?" asked Mr. Smirk.

"Can I please just move to the back row?" pleaded Lola.

"There's room next to me," Nassim offered as he smiled at Lola.

"Why not," responded Mr. Smirk.

Lola took what sounded like an endless breath and quickly ran to the back row.

Before all the kids could say "Cheese!" Mr. Smirk said, "Okay, boys and girls, straighten up and show me your best smiles!"

He peeked through his lens. There in front of him stood nine excited students showing off their missing-tooth grins . . . and one *BIG* red hat in the back row.

"You there in the corner, let me see your face. Please take off your hat," requested Mr. Smirk again, looking straight at Lola.

Lola could sense everyone's eyes focused on her like laser beams in a dark room. She felt icy cold, and her feet seemed like they were frozen to the ground.

"Just take off your hat," said Zach. "We want to see your face."

Suddenly, Omar, Mila, Ashwin, and Kate followed Zach's lead.

Before Lola knew it, a chorus of voices recited, "Take off your hat! Take off your hat! Take off your hat!"

Like an itch that won't go away, the chanting became so annoying that Lola just wanted it to *STOP*. Suddenly, Lola grabbed the rim of her hat and threw it across the floor. "There, now you can see my face covered in all these freckles," she said. "Can we finally take this picture now!"

The room filled with a loud silence. Lola felt like an animal in the zoo. If a miniature elephant in a pink tutu had danced into the gym at that moment, she wondered if anyone would've noticed.

Her heart pounded away like a drum. *BOOM. BAM. BOOM. BAM.*
"Just breathe," Lola whispered to herself.

There was something different about the way her classmates looked at her now. Lola felt it was the first time they had ever truly seen her.

"I have an idea!" said Nassim. "Come with me, Lola."
He stepped out of the back row and ran with Lola to their
backpacks. He whispered something in her ear that made
her grin. They both pulled out their pencil cases and
searched for a specific color.

"Ready!" called out Lola to Nassim.
"Everyone, please line up in front of
Lola and me," urged Nassim.

"I can't wait to see how this turns out," giggled Lola.

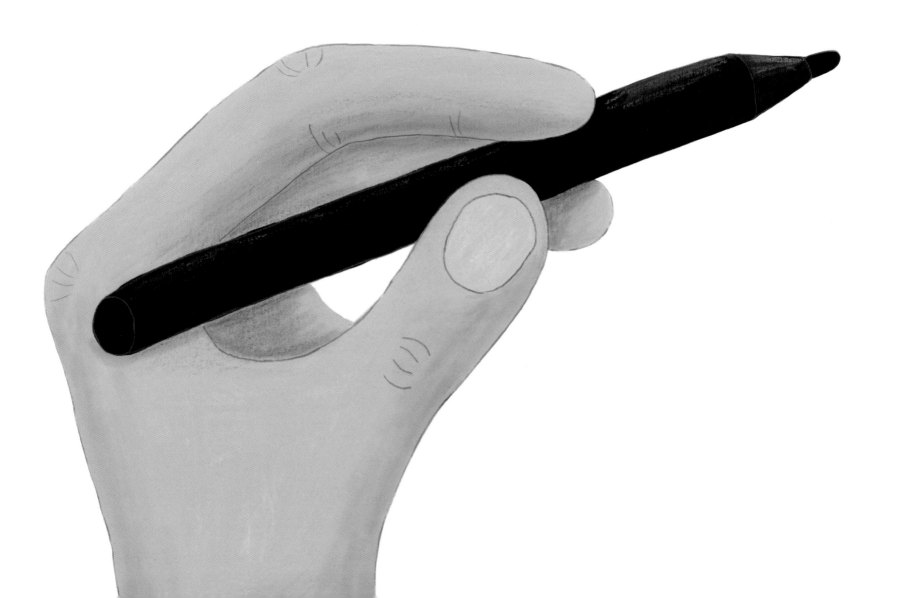

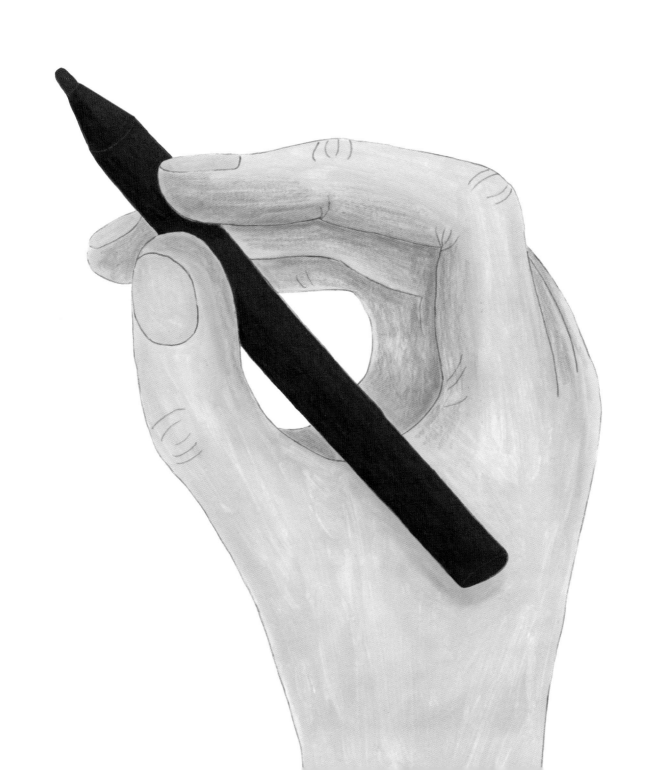

A few weeks later, all the kids in Ms. Sung's
class found an envelope on their desks.
"What's this?" asked Zach.
"I'm happy to announce that our class picture
has arrived," responded Ms. Sung.

"This year's photo is one-of-a-kind, so I have placed it
in a red frame. Where should we hang it up, class?"
Beaming with a smile, Ms. Sung held up the framed photo.

Lola didn't know what to say. *I can't believe they all did it,*
she thought. Her heart swelled with confidence and pride.
"Because of you, we now have this amazing class photo!" said Nassim.
"Thanks for sharing your great idea," responded Lola.
They gave each other a loud high-five.

Since then, Lola has celebrated her freckles because they're uniquely
hers. She now looks forward to picture day. She still wears her red hat
to school some days because it shelters her from both the chilly rain
and the hot sun. On other days, Lola leaves it at home and proudly
shows off her wonderfully freckled face.

To all children (and to myself):
be brave enough to love yourself.
– Xiaoyu

To the lovely you!
– Leying

Copyright © 2022 Clavis Publishing Inc., New York

Visit us on the Web at www.clavis-publishing.com.

No part of this publication may be reproduced or stored in a retrieval system,
or transmitted in any form or by any means, electronic, mechanical, photocopying,
recording, or otherwise, without the prior written permission of the publisher,
except in the case of brief quotations embodied in critical articles and reviews.
For information regarding permissions, write to Clavis Publishing, info-US@clavisbooks.com.

Peacock Is a Little Shy written by Xiaoyu Jin and illustrated by Leying Li

ISBN 978-1-60537-655-4

This book was printed in December 2021 at Nikara, M. R. Štefánika 858/25, 963 01 Krupina, Slovakia.

First Edition
10 9 8 7 6 5 4 3 2 1

Clavis Publishing supports the First Amendment and celebrates the right to read.

Written by Xiaoyu Jin
Illustrated by Leying Li

Peacock
Is a Little Shy

Clavis

NEW YORK

My peacock friends pop up their tails, one after the other.
They all can make perfect fans.
Everyone loves it, and my friends are proud of themselves.
Of course—it's a special moment for a peacock!
But I can't do it. I've never been able to display my tail.

Mom always says: "What beautiful feathers you have.
You should show them off!"

"Don't let your tail hang," Dad says.
"It looks best when it's open. Try it!"

Grandpa and Grandma encourage me as well:
"Come on, son, show us how handsome you are. You can do it!"

Everyone is looking forward to it.
But I'm not sure my tail will be as beautiful as everyone expects.

Sometimes, it can be overwhelming.
So, I go to the forest to visit my other animal friends.

Look! That's where Tortoise lives.
He seems pretty busy.

"The wind has blown all these leaves here.
I need to clean my house."

Tortoise moves very slowly.
One by one, he brings out the leaves.
At this rate, it's going to take him
an awfully long time to clean everything up.

Tortoise

Maybe I can help?
I'll just sweep my tail . . .

and the leaves are gone in no time.

"Thank you, Peacock!
What a beautiful and useful tail you have!"

Just down the road live my ant friends. It looks like it's moving day.
"Quick! Keep going! You, in the back, don't get left behind!"

But now it's raining. Thick drops make deep holes in the ground,
and soon a puddle blocks their path. The last group of ants can't get through.
"The river is too wide. There's no way we can cross it!"

For me, it's only a tiny river. No big deal!
I make a bridge for the ants with the long feathers of my tail.

They climb on and quickly cross to the other side of the water.
"Thank you, Peacock! What a soft and safe tail you have!"

I walk a little further.
Many of my bird friends live high up in the trees.
I can see them flying already.
But why is Grandpa Bird standing on that branch all by himself?

Oh . . . His nest has been broken by the rain.
The other birds are bringing twigs to build a new home for Grandpa.

I would like to help, too.
I think about how much everyone likes my feathers.
Maybe Grandpa Bird could use one to decorate his new nest!

I pluck out my prettiest feather. It hurts a little, but it doesn't matter.
As soon as I put the feather in the nest, it dances in the wind, like a little flag.
"Thank you, Peacock. Your shiny feather makes my nest so much nicer!"

The sun is going down. It's time to go home.
I turn around and look at my long tail.
It didn't open today, as usual, but it did help many friends.
And everyone thought it was very beautiful.

The sun's golden rays fall warmly on my feathers,
on Tortoise's shell, on all my friends, and, in the distance, on my family.
The rays are dazzling. I can barely keep my eyes open.

But then, when I'm almost home, I see the girl next door.
She's glowing in the sun's light. Her feathers, her eyes, her neck . . .
everything looks golden. How gorgeous!

At that moment, I feel my confidence growing.
After helping my friends in the forest, I feel I have more courage.
Enough courage to walk up to the beautiful girl.

But . . . why is everyone looking at me like that?

When I turn around, I can't believe my eyes.
That beautiful fan, it's mine! My tail is open!

Full of happiness, my parents run toward me.
I even see a tear in the corner of Mom's eye.
Yes, I did it!

I'm not afraid to show myself anymore.
To be myself. And even though one feather
is missing, I feel like I have the most
beautiful tail in the world!

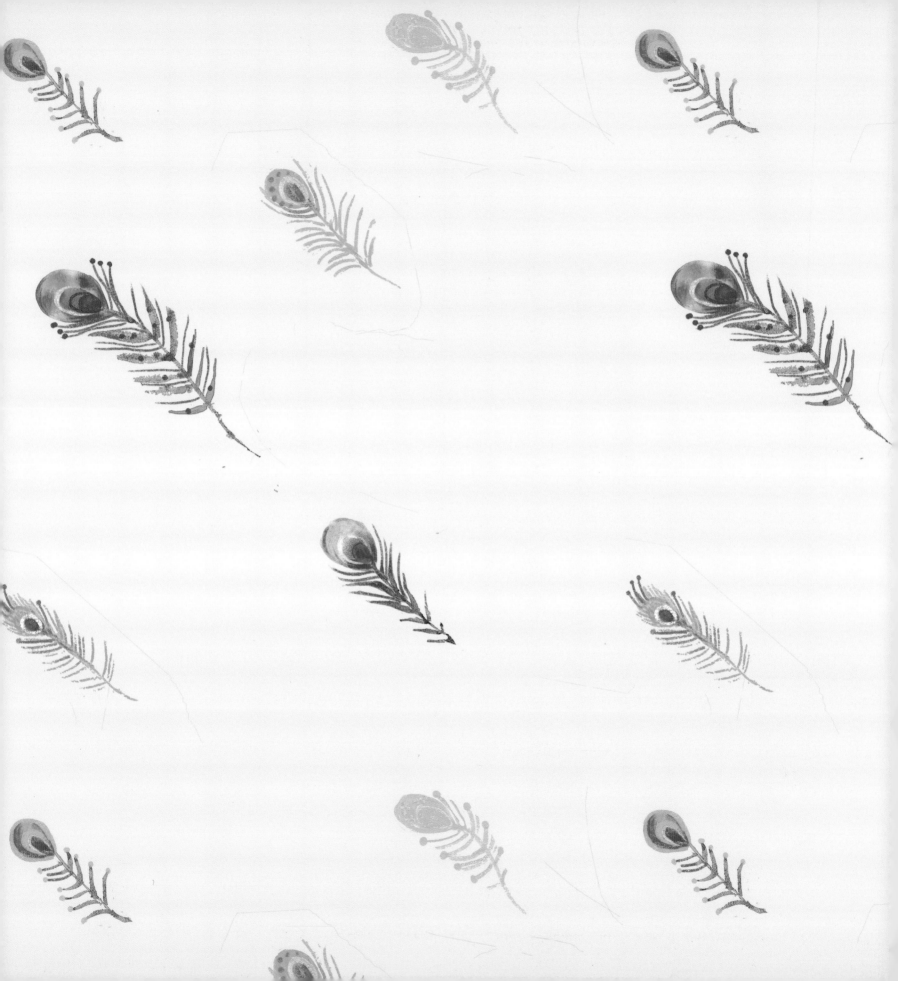